Louie

For Florence B. Freedman

PUFFIN BOOKS
Published by Penguin Group
Penguin Young Readers Group,
345 Hudson Street, New York, New York 10014, U.S.A.
Penguin Books Ltd, 80 Strand, London WC2R ORL, England
Penguin Books Australia Ltd, 250 Camberwell Road, Camberwell, Victoria 3124, Australia
Penguin Books Canada Ltd, 10 Alcorn Avenue, Toronto, Ontario, Canada M4V 3B2
Penguin Books (N.Z.) Ltd, 182-190 Wairau Road, Auckland 10, New Zealand

First published in the United States of America by Greenwillow Books, 1975
Published simultaneously by Viking and Puffin Books, divisions of Penguin Young Readers Group, 2004

10 9 8 7 6 5 4 3 2 1

Copyright © Ezra Jack Keats, 1975
All rights reserved

Library of Congress cataloging-in-publication data is available.
Puffin Books ISBN 0-14-240080-7

Manufactured in China

EZRA JACK KEATS

Louie

PUFFIN BOOKS

Susie and Roberto were putting on a puppet show.
They had spent a lot of time making the puppets.
Kids were trying to find seats next to their friends.
"Wow! Everybody's here!" said Susie.

"There's Louie," said Roberto.
"I never heard a word out of him."
"Me neither," said Susie.
"Well, let's get started."

The curtain opened.
A mouse puppet appeared on the stage.

The mouse introduced Gussie.
When Louie saw Gussie, he stood up.
"Hey, sit down!"
"We can't see through you, Louie!"
"C'mon, sit down, will ya?"
Louie just stood and stared.

"Hello!" he said.

"What's going on?" asked Susie.
  Roberto peeked over the stage.
"It's Louie!" he whispered.
"He's talking to Gussie. He won't stop.
  What'll we do?"
  Susie thought for a moment.
"We'd better have Gussie answer him."

"Hi, Louie," Susie said in Gussie's voice. "Nice to see you.
But me and the mouse gotta get on with the show.
Will you please sit down? There's lots more to come."
Louie sat down. The place got quiet
and the play continued. The kids
laughed at the adventures of
Gussie and the mouse.

When the show ended, the puppets bowed.
Everybody cheered and clapped.
Louie jumped up and clapped loudest and longest.

As everyone was leaving, Susie and Roberto saw Louie.

"Would you like to say good-bye to Gussie?" Susie asked.

Louie grabbed the puppet and held on to it.

"What'll I do now?" Susie whispered to Roberto.

"Gussie is very tired," explained Roberto.

"She has to go home now."

Louie waited a minute, then let go of Gussie.

Susie and Roberto started off.

Louie waved until they were out of sight.

Then he walked home.

He went into his room
and sat on the floor.

He dreamed he was feeding Gussie
from a huge ice-cream cone.

Suddenly Gussie disappeared! And the cone, too!

Louie was falling

down

down

down

Now he was floating.
There were kids all around.
They were making fun of him.
"Hello, hello!"
"Nah—it's good-bye, good-bye!"
"Oh, yeah—hello and good-bye, Louie!"

"Louie," his mother called.

"Louie," she called, "what are you doing?"
He didn't answer. He was still sad from his dream.
His mother went on, "Someone slipped a note
for you under the door. It says,

'Hello! Hello! Hello!
Go outside and follow
the long green string.'"

Louie got up and went outside.